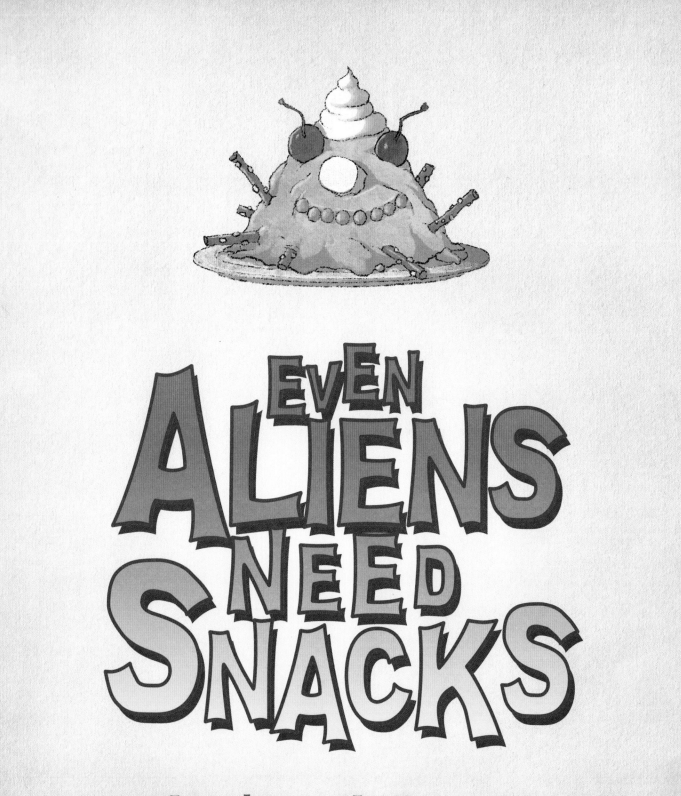

EVEN ALIENS NEED SNACKS

Matthew McElligott

WALKER BOOKS FOR YOUNG READERS
AN IMPRINT OF BLOOMSBURY
NEW YORK   LONDON   NEW DELHI   SYDNEY

To Christy, Anthony, Mom, Pop, and Gingie "Knuckles" Nice

First published in the United States of America in August 2012
by Walker Books for Young Readers, an imprint of Bloomsbury Publishing, Inc.
Paperback edition published in August 2014
www.bloomsbury.com

Bloomsbury is a registered trademark of Bloomsbury Publishing Plc

For information about permission to reproduce selections from this book, write to
Permissions, Walker BFYR, 1385 Broadway, New York, New York 10018
Bloomsbury books may be purchased for business or promotional use. For information on bulk
purchases please contact Macmillan Corporate and Premium Sales Department at
specialmarkets@macmillan.com

The Library of Congress has cataloged the hardcover edition as follows:
McElligott, Matthew.
Even aliens need snacks / Matthew McElligott.
p.   cm.
Summary: Creating snacks that make most humans queasy, a young chef finds a new clientele—aliens.
ISBN 978-0-8027-2398-7 (hardcover) • ISBN 978-0-8027-2399-4 (reinforced)
[1. Cooking—Fiction. 2. Extraterrestrial beings—Fiction. 3. Humorous stories.] I. Title.
PZ7.M478448Et 2012   [E]—dc23   2011050071

ISBN 978-0-8027-3652-9 (paperback)
ISBN 978-0-8027-3814-1 (e-book) • ISBN 978-0-8027-3815-8 (e-PDF)

Illustrations created with ink, pencil, and digital techniques
Typeset in Aunt Mildred
Book design by Nicole Gastonguay

Printed in China by Hung Hing Printing (China) Co., Ltd., Shenzhen, Guangdong
2 4 6 8 10 9 7 5 3 1

All papers used by Bloomsbury Publishing, Inc., are natural, recyclable products
made from wood grown in well-managed forests. The manufacturing processes
conform to the environmental regulations of the country of origin.

My mom is a great cook.
She always lets me help out
in the kitchen.

She even lets me make up my own recipes. Today I invented an eggplant, mustard, and lemonade smoothie. It's delicious.

My sister says it's disgusting.

She says that no one in the world
would eat the things I cook.

She says that no one in the whole
universe would eat the things I cook.

We'll see . . .

Hmmmph.

I knew my idea was good! I just
had the hours wrong.
I run back inside and get dressed.

My first customer is from out of town.

He really likes my mushroom iced tea. I think he even tries to pay me for it.

It doesn't take long before word
starts to spread.

As the summer goes by, I learn that
each customer has a favorite dish.

Some like my Swiss cheese donut holes.

Some like my turnip-side-down cake.

Some prefer sponge cake with leeks,

and bean puffs are especially popular
with the guys from the gas planets.

Even my toothpaste soup is a big hit.

But next week, school starts. It's time to close up for the summer.

I decide to try something special for my last night: a dessert made from every single one of my favorite ingredients.

I call it Galactic Pudding. It will be my masterpiece.

I open early. My customers
are already lined up.

They can't wait to try the pudding . . .

. . . and I can't wait to hear what
they think of it.

Well, *I* liked it.

I guess my sister was right.

There really are some things . . .

...no one else in the universe will eat.

Matthew McElligott is the author of many books for children, including *Even Monsters Need Haircuts*, *The Lion's Share*, and two Backbeard the Pirate adventures. He is not an alien, although he often eats like one. He is galactose intolerant.

www.mattmcelligott.com